A Special Couple

Hot Erotic Short Stories Illustrated with Hentai Pictures

_____

Emily White

TABLE OF CONTENTS

INTRODUCTION

Welcome to a captivating journey where my enthralling stories seamlessly intertwine with enchanting illustrations that redefine the very essence of desire in the world of hentai erotica.

Within the secret pages of these forbidden tales, I invite you to immerse yourself in a fiery universe of unrestrained passion. Every word is a whispered moan, and each illustration is a visual embrace that transforms the realms of fantasy into tangible reality.

This collection is not for the faint of heart. It's a bold manifesto, an invitation urging you to delve into the dark depths of lust, where pleasure is painted with audacious strokes and details that promise to quicken the rhythm of your heart. The illustrations are provocative gateways, guiding you into sensual dimensions where every hidden desire finds its expression without remorse.

Are you ready to plunge into a whirlwind of seduction and temptation, where the pages themselves transform into a stage for your most secret fantasies? Allow yourself to be carried away into a realm where sin transforms into art, and art seamlessly merges harmoniously with the ecstasy of desire.

Lift the cover and prepare for an experience ignited by the flame of passion. This is not just another collection; it's your exclusive ticket to the boldest manifestations of anime eros, written masterfully by me, **Emily White**.

GISÈLE

At the time we were 30 years old, Gisèle my wife 30 and me 31, a couple with a blossoming sexuality, but very conventional, and then one day, everything changed to our great satisfaction. We were invited to the wedding of one of my childhood friends. For this occasion, Gisèle had worn, once again, this dress that I must admit put me in all my states and that put her particularly in the spotlight. Gisèle was of an average height, with brown hair with some auburn highlights and a pleasant physique of which an imposing chest was generally preserved, which quite often attracted the male gaze and even more often the hands and mouth.

On this occasion, she wore a long black dress, with a rather wise décolletage showing only the beginning of her breasts, with thin straps but leaving a good half of her back uncovered, preventing her from wearing a bra. Well made up, with her hair pulled back into a bun, her outfit was completed by a pair of rather classic shoes. Thus dressed, she was able to see her seduction in my eyes, which were devouring her. On the way to the ceremony, I couldn't help but caress her thigh, devoid of tights or stockings, through the thin fabric of her dress. She prevented me from continuing my caress further, claiming that we would not linger at the party and that the night would be filled with promising embraces. I accepted the omen...

The ceremony went rather mundanely, followed by a vin d'honneur served in the garden on that balmy June evening. We realized that we didn't know many people at the party, so we decided to leave as soon as possible. Dinner started off pleasantly, and at times, either my leg or my wife's leg would go to the other, creating an atmosphere of complicity between us. When the DJ started playing, I naturally invited Gisèle to dance. I hugged her as much as possible, which allowed me to feel the warmth of her belly and breasts against me. A flirtation began between us:

You look beautiful tonight, you know, you make me want to go!

I think I'm doing it on purpose, after all, I have urges too...'.

Oh yeah, like what?

'For you to take off my dress and kiss me all over'.

Everywhere?

'Yes, everywhere, I also want to feel your hands everywhere'.

Everywhere?

Yes everywhere" 'And then what?

'And what else?'

'I want to feel your sex'

"'Everywhere?

'Oh yes, everywhere.

"'Even here?'

I said quietly letting my hand slide over her buttocks.

'Yes'

She answered in a huff and snuggled into me, leaving me in no doubt as to how she intended to end the evening. I was a little surprised though, because while she didn't reject this type of penetration in the slightest, she wasn't an unconditional fan of sodomy either. I attributed this desire to the disturbance of feeling unusually nearly naked under her light clothes.

Now we were close enough and I was sure to caress her bare back, her waist, the hollow of her loins to the edge of the only underwear she wore. My hand went around her side, down to her waist. Sensing my intentions, she passed her hands around my neck, thus freeing access to one of her breasts whose underside my fingertips could now caress. For her part, she swayed slightly against me, her belly attached to mine, caressing the nape of my neck, amused by the turmoil she was causing in me and whose physical manifestation she could not ignore.

'My dear, I think I'm having an effect on you, if this keeps up we'll have trouble getting home' she said.

You're right, in fact I'm seriously thinking of stopping along the way.

What do you mean?

To find a quiet place, a small road, a parking lot, and so on.

And for what?" she asked, falsely quizzical

'I don't know, do you know a nice woman with a friendly mouth?

'Oh yes.'

'And where is she?'

'In your arms... until you're better...'.

The deal seemed done, and I was already waiting for her lips, whose sweetness I knew, and her tongue, whose skill I knew.

On the way back to our house we passed the groom arguing with one of his friends, whom he introduced to us, informing us both of our shared taste in computers.

The conversation began with Patrick who, in addition to being friendly, had an interesting and not humorless storage. I still saw him as an intruder who would surely delay our departure, who prevented me from enjoying Gisèle and also surprised him at times, not without a mixture of pride and annoyance, by looking at his bust.

He began a series of slowdowns and of course asked my permission to invite Gisèle to dance, which I could only grant him. They pulled away and started dancing. At one point, my gaze fell on the dancing couple and, no! I couldn't dream, Patrick's hand seemed to go over Gisele's rear end. As I looked more closely, I noticed that the hands were often changing positions on her bare back, but also a little lower. From my seat I could see that my wife didn't seem to notice anything and seemed to be enjoying the conversation of her escort who was talking to her very closely.

In fact, early in our marriage, I had noticed that Gisele was particularly aroused during our intercourse when we had previously watched a pornographic film with groups of male and female participants and perhaps more specifically scenes in which a woman was engaged with several partners. We eventually talked about it, admitting that it must be exciting to have group sex in front of her husband and me admitting that I would love to see her indulge in other men in front of me; she was, at the time, more reluctant to see me in the company of another woman, although she was favorably considering intimacy with another woman.

Then we never had the opportunity to fulfill these various fantasies, which were buried deep in our memories for several years, only to resurface today.

They finished dancing and I noticed that a certain blush colored Gisèle's face, who seemed quite silent. Patrick, on the other hand, seemed very comfortable. In turn, I invited my partner to dance. Immediately, she squeezed me tightly, finally admitting that she was wet because of Patrick who had subjected her to a full-blown groping session. Crushing her breasts against my chest, she admitted with great shame that not only had she not dared or wanted to put a stop to Patrick's actions, but that she had finally found pleasure in them. I placed one thigh between hers so that she could press her pubic bone against it and asked her:

'It looks like you're a priest to take the plunge?'

What do you mean?" she replied in a hypocritical tone.

Doing what we've always talked about but never found an opportunity for, I'm sure Patrick finds you very attractive.

Do you think he does? It scares me a little, you know.

I'm sure if you let yourself go, everything will be fine, especially in the state you're in."

She agreed and I added

And don't worry, I'll be there."

'Happy again' she replied

I was about to reply that I thought she was a little greedy when the DJ announced the now famous classic:

'And now, a date change'.

As if by magic, the inevitable Patrick was next to us and after a complicit look with Gisele, I gave up my seat to him. This time I watched them closely. He had hugged Gisele quite tightly and she wasn't running away from the embrace. He had put his arms around her shoulders, leaving her entire body at the mercy of his hands. The latter, feeling no reluctance, seemed to push his advantage, caressing her waist, her hips, her bare back without restraint, even sliding his fingers inside her dress or letting his hands go to the bottom of her loins or even lower. At one point, with Gisèle's back to me, I could no longer see Patrick's hands, so I concluded that he must have started on her breasts. During this time, he spoke in her ear, after which she told me that having realized the matter was settled, he had complimented her on her physique and the way he would like to use it. It seemed to me that she turned her lips away from a kiss that might have been considered improper by the other guests. They stopped dancing and Patrick, holding Gisele by the waist, came over to join me.

Gisele just told me that you would be willing to try a group experience.

That's right, isn't it, honey?

Yes, it's the first time, maybe we're not used to it.

He reassured us, confessing that he and his girlfriend (who was not among the guests) were part of a swinger's group in the town where they lived at the other end of France. He then invited us to follow him to the room he had booked in the same hotel where the party was taking place. After a last look exchanged with Gisèle, which seemed to seal the fate, I told her about our agreement. The die was cast...

As soon as we reached his room, he drew Gisèle against him, gave her a light kiss on the lips that she did not refuse, then two, then three and looking her in the eyes, he took possession of her mouth where he met an agile and flexible tongue that came to meet hers. This scene continued to excite me, it was the first time I had ever seen another man kiss my wife, and I went to stroke my wife's back and buttocks. Patrick moved back a little, then put his hands on her bare shoulders and continuing to look her in the eyes began to slide the thin straps.

When her shoulders were free, Gisele lowered her arms to her sides and slowly the dress slid to the floor. He put an arm around her shoulders and kissed her for a long time, caressing one breast with his free hand. Slowly he swung her over to me and placed his hands under her breasts as if to weigh them, then grabbing the erect buds with his thumbs and index fingers he reached out and rolled them under his fingers. Under the treatment, she emitted a moan that didn't surprise me, knowing the sensitivity of the fleshy globes she was attacking. I leaned in for a kiss, which she eagerly returned, obviously very excited. As I kissed her, I slid a hand inside her panties toward her silky pubic area. The wetness of the thin fabric told me her state of arousal and staring into her now slightly misty eyes, I began to slide the last piece of clothing down her sides.

She was naked. Turning her head, she let Patrick kiss her and I could follow the ballet of their tongues wrapping around each other. Responding to my request, she spread her legs slightly and opened her crotch to me, where I could caress her clit. Groaning, she leaned back against my arm, inviting my hand to continue its path. I slipped a finger into the lips of her sex, then penetrated her soaked vagina, a second finger came to help the first to offer her the pleasure her moans demanded, my other hand titillating her stinging clit. Soon under the action of four hands that took care of her breasts and her groin Gisele contracted in a spasm of pleasure of which I collected the evidence on my fingers. Patrick turned her around in front of him and, weighing her on his shoulders, made my wife understand that he, in turn, intended to benefit from her favors. Slowly, he knelt down, unzipped his underpants, quickly pulled down his briefs, which revealed a member swollen with desire that she began to gently caress with one hand, while the other weighed his swollen testicles.

Don't make me pry," she breathed.

As if in a dream, I saw Gisele moisten her lips with a lascivious movement of her tongue, then begin to lick the glans that was offered to her with circular movements of her tongue, and then, her eyes fixed on Patrick's, as if to observe his reactions, she kissed the straining penis.

Patrick let out a long grunt of pleasure and then finished undressing while Gisele continued to suck him with application. I could see her lips sliding, her cheeks deepening, engulfing, sucking the member, her tongue sliding over it, her hands caressing it. In turn, I let go of my clothes and moved closer to them. Seeing my imposing erection, Gisèle abandoned the sex she was enjoying to greedily swallow mine. For a while, she alternated between sucking one, masturbating the other, switching from one sex to the other with ecstasy, alternating deep sucks with kinky licks. In amazement, I noticed that he was taking intense pleasure in manipulating the taut rods, swallowing them with rapture.

Unable to bear it any longer, I escaped from her lips, to give myself some respite. Patrick took the opportunity to make her get up, drag her onto the bed or make her lie down, he opened her thighs widely and after caressing her vulva with his sex, he penetrated her with a powerful stroke of his kidneys. Under the ardor of the penetration, she let escape a moan of pleasure and, following her rhythm to that of her lover, tied her legs around his waist. After a bit of back and forth, he lifted her legs to place them on his shoulders and thus pierce her deep, which seemed to give her intense pleasure. I was still a little surprised to see Gisèle giving herself without restraint, offering her tongue to the one who was searching her mouth, going along with the blows he was inflicting on her without any care, even letting herself go to ask for more.

Yes, come on, ... harder, ... give me big blows .... Yes, again ... I'm leaving!

And as she did so, I saw her twitch, with a soft cry accompanying her first orgasm. Far from satisfying her, this first pleasure seemed to have aroused her and as Patrick slowly resumed his thrusts she reached out to grab my member. When Patrick saw it, he withdrew from her cum-soaked vagina, but not without provoking his partner's dismayed protest:

Oh no, stay...

Wait, you'll see, get on all fours, yes like that, spread your thighs, good ... Philippe will take you doggy style."

She got into the position indicated, I went behind her and in turn penetrated her sex made very welcoming by the previous penetration and the abundance of secretions due to her excitement. I grabbed her by the hips and began to slowly but thoroughly file her as I knew she liked it.

Patrick went around the bed, placed one knee on it and presented a turgid, wet, glistening member in front of her face. After a moment's hesitation she began to lick Patrick's glans, who interrupted her:

'Come on, suck it, don't make a fuss, you'll see, he's got taste now'.

And taking hold of her sex she forced (oh so very little) lips rounding around her sex stained with vaginal secretion. For the first time in her life, Gisèle was faced with two partners possessing her at the same pace, each penetration throwing her in front of the meat gag. She went faster and faster in the face of my thrusts and a second orgasm shook her intensely unleashing in me a tenfold pleasure of an unusual abundance. Aware that she had abandoned him for a few moments, Gisele resumed her fellatio. Patrick cupped his hand in my wife's hair and warned her:

This is it, take it all!" and he ejaculated into her surrounding mouth. I felt Gisele swallow and pump the stinger down to the last drop. Patrick withdrew from her indulgent mouth and as he complimented her on her sucking skills, he grabbed a bottle of champagne from the mini-bar and served us a glass.

We sat on the bed, Gisele between us, and, I'd say almost naturally, as we drank we began stroking her back, her shoulders, her thighs, our fingers playing with the curls of her pubes. Drawing her to me, I kissed her for a long time, then it was Patrick's turn. He moved from one mouth to the other, offering his tongue, sucking ours, having his lips bitten or sucked. During this time, our hands did not remain idle, and it is above all his proud breasts that took the brunt of the operation soupesés, caressed, kneaded, he offered us his chest with dardés nipples that were now a dark red color by dint of having been rolled triturés, pinched, stretched ...

She had taken a member in each hand and was trying to restore our desired virility. We turned her over on the bed and started sucking her breasts making her moan with pleasure, leaving the fleshy globes to Patrick, I slipped between Gisele's legs, opened her thighs and parted the lips of her sex and started licking her dripping pussy. I introduced two fingers into her intimacy and focused my oral practice on her clit. When a third finger was added to the others, her hips began to undulate frantically, she arched her back violently and flooded the masturbating fingers with her orgasm, which I withdrew from the cavity where they had been inserted to give her to lick - pretty much everything, although she didn't seem to hate it....

We then decided to switch roles, Patrick took over the crotch and passing over my wife, I slid my penis between her breasts inviting her to masturbate me between her milky globes, which she did as she licked her lips for a future invitation.

At one point I saw a brief glimmer of annoyance in her eyes, then things returned to normal and I lay on my side with my sex level with her lips which immediately surrounded my glans.

At that moment Patrick manifested his intention to sodomize Gisèle and I realized only at that moment that two of his fingers were nestled in the desired duct to probably enlarge its diameter, and of course I understood that it was this penetration that seemed to have upset him. To my surprise, he pushed me away and then obediently got into position, first on all fours, then leaning against the bed, his back arched, rump raised high, waiting for the announced penetration. I was amazed at my docility and Patrick asked:

It doesn't bother you at all."

Considering what had already happened during the evening, I could only reply negatively, regretting that it was to him that Gisèle was offering her kidneys and indicating that she was not a great habitué.

Don't worry, everything will be fine," he said.

He finished lubricating the grommet with the product of Gisele's crotch, then walked over to the tight target and pressed the glans against the corolla. Slowly I watched the member sink into the distended anus. I could finally witness the spectacle of my partner's sodomization before my eyes, which I must admit is one of my favorite fantasies. Despite the precautions taken the ring held out and I could hear my wife panting under the strain. Patrick asked me to masturbate her to get her to relax, which I did with one hand while the other worked on her chest. Suddenly she let out a small cry and Patrick sighed with satisfaction; the sphincter had finally given way. The rest of the penetration was easier and I saw his sex slowly but steadily penetrate my wife's buttocks. He gave her time to adjust and then withdrew to penetrate her again, this time non-stop and thoroughly. The sheath being fitted to the imposed diameter, he took her by the hips and began a continuous coming and going that filled her.

Turning, she offered him her lips which he eagerly took. Then he grabbed her breasts with his hands and made her come and go, making her moan with pleasure. Seeing her being sodomized and seemingly experiencing great pleasure sent me over the edge and unable to hold her back any longer I sank into her open mouth where I poured in long jets that she couldn't fully absorb and that smeared her chin. Patrick was now pistoning her without restraint with a big back stroke as Gisele responded by projecting herself in front of the cock that was hitting her. Then she froze and in an unbroken moan she blew

Yes, yes, I will come.

Where do you come from?" he asked her

'From behind, oh yes it's hard, I'll come from behind.

Tell me that you're going to come from your ass'.

'Aaaah, I'm going to come from my ass'

'ah I can't take it anymore either, I'll give it all to you'.

'You're huge, give it all to me' and together they let out a moan of pleasure, she arched her back to the maximum and he arched his back, flooding her insides.

As soon as he let go a little, he withdrew, leaving Gisèle's anus wide open, from which the whitish liquid flowed slowly, the last witness of the pleasure he had taken.

After a short rest and a few kisses, we decided to take our leave of Patrick, and after a few last caresses and kisses on Gisèle's body, she put on her dress, neglecting to put her panties back on, and we made our way back.

***

After the first threesome, we talked about what had happened, the fulfillment of this shared fantasy, and Giselle told me about the confused feeling she had, a mixture of shame at having misbehaved and a strangely high level of arousal. She eventually confessed to me that she wouldn't be averse to another such adventure if the opportunity arose, as neither of us currently wished to try our luck with an ad or a dating club.

Since this initiation, I was pleased to note that many things had evolved with Gisèle, her skirts were a little shorter or a little more split, her blouses a little more recessed, one more button undone, her heels a little higher. I was also happy to see that thongs had reappeared in her wardrobe, as had stockings and suspenders. Her demeanor had also changed, when we were alone sometimes she would stay naked or put on just a pair of self-locking stockings or garters. We had wonderful moments that ended in passionate hugs.

We were celebrating the anniversary of our meeting a few days before and Gisele asked me:

For our anniversary, do you want me to get sexy?

Of course I said yes;

Well, I'll do some shopping, but you won't see the results until Saturday," she added mischievously.

She commandeered the bathroom for a long time that day. Curiously, I waited in another room. This patience was rewarded by the sight of the beautiful woman who appeared. A superb figure dressed all in black, high heels, short tailor's skirt, cleverly made up with a particularly well defined mouth. She slowly slipped off her suit jacket and turned to be admired before facing me again. In passing, as she surely desired, I could see that her stockings were seamed, something she knew I loved, and loved to follow from the ankle to places that promised pleasure. The blouse she wore was made of sheer black nylon and revealed her proud breasts, which were revealed almost to the halo by a black balconette bra that was more like a fan than an undergarment.

I tried to approach her, complimenting her beauty and pointing out that we were in no hurry, but she gently pushed me away, saying that a little waiting would only increase our pleasure. I reluctantly accepted the argument and we set off for our chosen restaurant. In the car she did nothing to hide her legs that her skirt revealed, and I couldn't help but put an exploratory hand on her bare thighs. My hand went up to the edge of the stocking and I stroked the bare skin with my fingertips, unable to pursue my advantage further due to the tightness of the skirt that would have to be rolled up to reach my extremities.

We arrived early and I parked in the restaurant parking lot and asked her:

Will you do me a favor?

This is our night, of course I want to please you."

'Then take off your panties.'

I knew I was costing her some money since she said she wasn't a fan of 'no panties'.

In a very erotic gesture she pulled up her skirt with difficulty, slipped a hand under it to catch the edge of the bulky panties and then lifting herself slightly released her pelvis from the grip of the underwear and slid it down her legs. She handed it to me and said, "It's a shame though, look how beautiful it was."

I grabbed a nice see-through thong I had purchased for the occasion and walked to the car to open the door for her. Of course she took her time getting out, making sure to spread her legs, stopping even when they were most open.

We took our seats at the table reserved for us and while we were enjoying our aperitif I asked her with a knowing look:

"Don't you think it's a little hot in here?"

"You don't want me to take off my jacket," she replied as she saw me coming.

"And why not, you're the one who wanted to be hot."

"Okay, okay," she agreed.

After a moment's hesitation she unbuttoned and left the superfluous garment behind. In the dim light she looked beautiful. Her well-defined lips were a constant invitation and she would occasionally run the tip of her tongue over her upper lip in a silent proposition and, most importantly, I found it hard to take my eyes off her almost half-naked breasts thinking that at the first sudden movement on her part a breast would come out of its place. She intercepted my gaze and with a naughty glint began to breathe deeply, making her curves swell to (almost) maximum.

I leaned over to her to tell her of the excitement she was causing me and was actually giving me a terrible boner. She added:

I hope so, I'm doing everything I can for this, I'm going to turn you on until you can't take it anymore."

In fact he continued his seduction maneuvers for a while, which he could see were successful in my eyes.

And then, under some pretext, salt, fire? I really don't know, the neighbors at the table next to ours started talking. I immediately noticed, a little annoyed, that both of them had, for my taste, rather enveloping, even insistent, looks towards my wife. I also noticed that she hadn't noticed this little maneuver as she continued her little breathing game from time to time. I still wondered, given their lack of discretion, if she wasn't pretending not to have noticed anything and trying, by arousing them, to make me a little jealous to increase my desire.

As the meal was coming to an end, they told us they knew of a nice club and asked if we wanted to go with them. We exchanged, as if time seemed to stand still, a look in which many expressions passed, strangeness of this proposal from a stranger, then complicity, anticipating a result full of sensuality, and still desire and apprehension of perhaps the beginning of a new adventure? Complicity, with a prospect of adventure that seemed to prevail, we accepted. Gisèle got up and went to the bathroom to put on her makeup. I caught the two men exchanging a knowing wink. A little disconcerted, not wanting to be dependent, I suggested they take my car. During the drive, which took three quarters of an hour, our new acquaintances, Michel and Jean Luc, competed in humor to brighten the time of transportation during which I anxiously and impatiently wondered what would happen and how. We arrived at a nightclub that was unfamiliar to us, of course, dim lights, a dance floor surrounded by small intimate booths. Michel and Jean Luc seemed to know the place well and guided us to one. Michel went to order drinks and I took the opportunity to invite Gisèle to dance.

After a few seconds of silence he asked: if I understood correctly, if I interpreted your look and read your thoughts correctly, you would like me to be fucked by these two guys, wouldn't you?

I would? I would? Would you want to?

I don't know.

'Don't you like them? But I thought I read what was going on in your little head too?

'Oh that's not it, I'm not bad?

'So you don't want to make love, is that it?

You almost made me undress in front of the whole restaurant, you can imagine it had an effect on me too, I'm in a state. Tell me frankly, do you want to see me make love to them?

Yes, I would love to see you with them, I loved it the first time.

'Yes, but now there are two of them and they seem like fun people for parties.

'Anyway, it's your decision, you're the one who will be taken, you decide'.

She hugged me and said:

'I'm a little nervous, but we said we would do it again, maybe this is our chance, but maybe they don't expect it from us.

Oh well, I don't think so, you saw the way they looked at you, I'm cool, and besides, you can always provoke them if you see they don't have the desired reactions, besides didn't you deprive yourself of that at the restaurant?

We returned to our seats and toasted with Michel and Jean Luc who toasted to Gisèle's charm.

Jean Luc invited my partner to dance and I stayed alone with Michel watching what was happening on the dance floor. It seemed to me that the atmosphere of the club had changed a bit. Couples of dancers were moving around the dance floor, men were openly caressing their partners, women were offering themselves to these caresses and even doing some rather daring ones on or in their partner's fly. One woman had even let her date open her blouse and was dancing topless.

Michel explained to me that the club was getting hotter and hotter as the night went on and that it was a meeting place for swingers, he also added that it was a swingers club by showing me a tent at the back of the room. Then he said:

'You're really lucky, Gisele is a beautiful woman, you don't have to get bored with her' and when I nodded he added:

You wouldn't be here, we would have tried to seduce her and abuse her.

And why does my presence bother you?" I replied, to her surprise, wanting to shake things up a bit.

Oh you? you would be complacent and complicit? and Gisèle agrees? Tell me, are you used to this sort of thing?

Used is a big word, it only happened to us once and I think my wife liked it enough.

And would you like to do it again, to see your wife taken in front of you?

I think so, but let me ask you a question, you just told me that you would try to seduce her, you always try to flirt with two people.

Yes, some women, when they are well on their way, like to be taken by two partners who take turns making them come.

He continued quickly:

If you don't mind, we could try Gisele. She could be very, very interesting and, as I said, she has everything to please. She seems to have what it takes where it's needed" and added "and then, I'm sure you'd like to see your wife offer herself to us as a whore, if you don't mind, we'll get her a little wild?

I gave him my consent but was a little hesitant about my wife's reactions, an objection he quickly brushed off by saying 'Don't worry I'm sure she's very sexy and will enjoy it. We'll do anything to her,' and he continued.

I'm going to tell Jean Luc the good news," he said as he stood up, "and to Gisele, of course, who knows what she's doing, right?" he said a little mockingly and walked over to the couple.

Meanwhile, Jean Luc had not been idle. Of course, he had hugged Gisele quite tightly, and then chatted him up quite skillfully like a perfect seducer, with some slightly sketchy but very real caresses. My wife allowed herself to be seduced without any resistance, giving her silent consent to his actions. Then they saw Michel coming towards them. He put his arm around Gisèle's waist and said

I just had a great conversation with Philippe, my friend! The evening will probably be lively, it seems that Gisele is recently a follower of the male plurality, we could perhaps make her have a torrid evening" he said looking at Gisele who, upset, felt herself blushing.

For a short while they stayed like that, one holding her and the other holding her by the waist. She admitted later that she felt particularly vulnerable at that moment but very aroused between the two men. Then Michel added,

You introduced me to Gisèle, change partners!

So my wife changed partners. He drew her against him, told her about our conversation, joked that I had told him about our previous adventure, and reassured her that they would do their best to make sure she had an unforgettable evening and that they would take turns making sure she had maximum pleasure. He felt her soften against him and as he did so he could no longer ignore the erection he was unleashing.

Do you feel the effect you're having on me," he asked.

She answered in the affirmative and told him that if I wasn't there he would drag her into the bathroom, make her press on the toilet, tie her up and take her like that and that after that Jean Luc would take over.

You would have let him do that.

Maybe, I don't know...' she replied

Noticing the bare-breasted woman, he asked her if she had ever done the same thing in a public place. As she answered in the negative, while caressing them, placing her hand on one of them, he shamelessly proposed to bare her opulent breasts. She refused and they danced for a while longer with Michel kissing her on the neck. Gisèle, feeling that she could not refuse his lips for long, wanted to join Jean Luc and me. A hand placed on her buttocks escorted her back and made her sit between them.

We toasted once more, but this time to the rest of the evening. Then there was a slight awkwardness, which Jean Luc dispelled by having the drinks renewed and Michel then suggested a game:

"I propose a game.

A game?" I asked

Yes, for example, guess the color of Gisèle's panties".

The game will be over soon, she took it off when she entered the restaurant," I commented, staring into my wife's eyes to catch a blurry glint of desire. I immediately added, knowing I was rushing things, "Can you check it out?

Michel looked at me nodding and asked Gisèle.

'That's right, I can check, can't I?

I saw her swallow her saliva, lower her eyes and answer in the affirmative. Michel put his hand over Gisele's knee and then began to caress her thigh, which was uncovered by her skirt. Then his hand began a slow climb under her skirt. To facilitate his companion's progression, Jean Luc at the same time, pulled up her skirt that let the lower limit of her panties appear.

Continuing his maneuver, he told her:

Don't be shy, open your thighs?

Michel's hand slid along the inside of her thighs, which now opened slightly to allow her to advance. This hand had now reached the upper limit of the stocking and lingered for a moment on this edge, playing with the lacing of the garter. Jean Luc rolled up her skirt again and asked me to order Gisele to spread her legs wider so that we could all enjoy the show. I didn't ask and she complied, leaning against the backrest, breathing heavily, eyes closed, seeming to wait for the final contact. Jean Luc complimented her taste.

'Hummm, very nice, I love women who wear stockings, especially without panties' he said

Meanwhile Michel caressed the bare skin over the stockings, then touched the silky curls and his fingers reached their goal. Gisèle stiffened slightly at this moment and then seemed to abandon herself completely to the hand that was taking possession of her groin. Michel then told us:

'I checked, so it's true, Gisèle is not wearing panties, stockings? no panties? hmm, she was ready for adventure'.

Not completely," Jean Luc added, "she had a bra on.

Take it off," I suggested

Without hesitating, he put his hand on her breast, which he caressed through the transparent veil, then one by one he undid the buttons of her blouse and opened the flaps, telling her:

I will put them in the air, it will be easier for you to feel them."

Gisele, with her head tilted back, answered nothing and Jean Luc unfastened the laces of the cups, then passing a hand behind her back, snapped the clasp of her bra which she then easily removed. He unbuttoned the bodice down to the skirt, spread its sides and took one breast in his hand. With his other arm, he wrapped his arms around her shoulders and drew her face toward him to kiss her. Gisèle could not resist the world and I contemplated my wife, with her skirt rolled up, her thighs open, her blouse open, her breasts exposed, being caressed by one, offering her mouth greedily to the other who was groping her at the same time without restraint and all this in a public place... I was in a state of incredible excitement. Then it was Michel's turn who took possession of her lips for, the right word is, a monstrous skate that she returned with her tongue. Then she went from one mouth to the other until she had her first orgasm under the influence of intimate caresses. Turning to me, Michel suggested.

'We could finish the evening at my place, we would be more comfortable there to have fun with Gisele'.

I saw in his eyes, with their perverse glow, what the word 'fun' could mean, and in my wife's eyes a mixture of desire and anxiety. Of course, everyone agreed with this proposition. She withdrew her fingers from her soaked vagina, gave them to Jean Luc to sniff, who looked on approvingly and exclaimed:

Well, well, well, we won't be bored!

Michel then asked my wife to lick her fingers, then they untied her blouse from her skirt, picked it up and buttoned it in the back, leaving her chest completely bare, saying:

See, you too, now show them.

To get her jacket, she had to walk through the club in this attire, where the atmosphere was now totally unrestrained. Jean Luc told me that the evening would end with an incredible orgy behind the curtain, he also told me that if Gisele liked, in the afternoon, the entrance was free for single women and couples, and that those who arrived there had no time to get bored, I noted this information in the corner of my head.

When I got to the car, I took the wheel, with Michel next to me and Jean Luc and Gisèle behind, where he started driving. I saw in the rearview mirror that he had asked her to take off her jacket, that he was kissing her breasts and then her mouth. He had also rolled up her skirt and in turn had definitely taken possession of her crotch.

Michel had turned around to enjoy the show and after a few hundred yards, he protested that it wasn't fair that only Jean Luc was taking advantage of Gisèle and asked me to stop while he got in the back seat. As a formality, I asked Gisèle for her consent.

'Do you want Michel to go with you in the back?

'Yes,' she replied in a whisper.

I parked, Michel got out, sat next to her and the boxing session began again. Kissed, licked, masturbated, at one point wanted to roll up her skirt completely to expose her buttocks. The tightness of the garment made their plan impossible.

We'll take it off completely, but you've been warned that if we take it off, you'll have to go bare-assed in the street, right?

I heard Gisele answer in a white voice.

The sound of a zipper and in the mirror I saw her complacently lift herself up to allow them to slip the garment off.

'Now you're more comfortable, go ahead and spread your thighs, yes, that's it, run them over our legs, oh it's wet, two fingers, like in butter, here, wait, I'll put a third one on you so you'll feel better, here' exclaimed Jean Luc as Michel kneaded her breasts as he kissed her. The trip was getting tiring and I was speeding up. Without a care in the world, Gisèle let herself go, moaning. Michel had placed a hand behind her back and was probably starting to slide into the cleft of her buttocks. A curious middle finger positioned itself on her anus, trying to enter. The jerking of the car and the treatment they were giving her caused the ring to yield easily to digital penetration.

Well, she fits well on that side too, do you fuck her often?

From time to time, yes, especially when she's hot," I replied.

What about tonight, are you hot?" he asked her. She admitted, "Yes, she felt hot," to which he let slip a "Well, well! The thought of my wife being sodomized again by a stranger (or two) made my erection ache. And so, doubly masturbated, she took her pleasure again.

"You'll have to take care of us too," Michel said, "here, take my cock, then you can suck it for us.

And mine too," Jean Luc added. He didn't have time to perform the required fellatio because one of the two said 'ah dommage on est arrivé!

I parked, stopped the engine and turned around to contemplate the scene of what was my wife and she was offering herself without restraint, no skirt, thighs open to the fingers that were masturbating her front and back, blouse completely open, breasts in the air, disheveled, manipulating a sex in each of her hands. We got out of the car, something promised, something owed, my buttocks in the air and undressed for Gisèle whom I finally drew against me to kiss her passionately as Michel opened the door to his pavilion.

Once inside, I removed her blouse leaving her in a low garter belt and heels.

She whispered to me:

I'm ashamed, but I'm in a state," she whispered, her eyes sparkling with excitement.

The moment of truth was imminent.

'I think you're going to have a hell of a night,' I said, caressing her bottom.

Don't worry, she'll get it, look," Jean Luc warned, undressing in a flash and showing a good-sized erect penis. He approached and she took him in her hand.

Suck me," he told her, "and apply yourself," he added, putting pressure on her shoulder. She obediently knelt down and after giving me a confused look, took the offered member. Michel and I took turns undressing and made a circle around Gisèle. Gisèle began a rotating fellatio, sucking one and masturbating the other two, trading erect limbs in front of her. Those of her two new partners were well endowed by nature and their cocks were, I must admit with frustration, much larger than mine which did not seem to displease, on the contrary, my dear and tender little wife who opened her mouth wide in order to receive them and pass from one to the other. They complimented her on her 'pipe-cutting skills' and added that with a little more practice 'she would be perfect'.

Then Michel interrupted her in her oral activities to drag her to the living room table where he had her lie on her back, lifted her legs which he held open, pointed his sex at Gisèle's entrance and penetrated her completely in one thrust. She let out a moan of pleasure that was quickly stifled by the penis that Jean Luc immediately inserted into her mouth. I positioned myself in front of him so that, by turning my head to the right and left, she could take turns between our lips while Michel penetrated her hard. After a few moments of this possession Michel said to me:

You might want to fuck her while your wifey sucks us off?

I answered in the affirmative and he withdrew to give me the seat made incredibly cozy by the excitement she had been held in all evening and the previous penetration. Michel had taken my place and I could see my wife masturbating and sucking both chucks with pleasure as her two lovers kneaded her breasts mercilessly. Suddenly I felt her pelvis go into a frenzy, the warm sheath of her sex contracting around my penis and flooding her with its stream of pleasure.

More? More? More? Yes," she moaned, cumming.

Her contractions had the effect of accelerating my own climax and I in turn achieved intense pleasure. Jean Luc got her off the table, then put her on all fours on the floor and took her doggy style with his hands gripping her hips. Michel had regained possession of her mouth. Each stroke of Jean Luc's pushed her onto Michel's outstretched cock asking Jean Luc:

What do you prefer, pussy or mouth?

Let's stay as we are, I'll get a blow job later.

'Okay, then slow down a bit, I'll rinse her mouth'.

Jean Luc held his sex deep and stopped his pacing, Michel took the opportunity to savor the know-how of Gisele who was sucking him with application. With a dull roar, he announced his orgasm. Gisèle tightened her lips around his member so as not to let out a drop, as she often did with me. Then Michel withdrew, she began to slowly swallow the semen that filled her mouth. She couldn't finish her tasting because Jean Luc had started pounding her violently, making her cry out, which made some cum drip down her chin.

The two lovers had a final orgasm almost simultaneously, which they expressed aloud. Under the excitement produced by the situation, we had not really relaxed, and Michel proposed to "continue the party". He sat down in an armchair and invited Gisèle to impale herself on him with her back to him. She straddled him, put her sex in line with her partner's and slowly let herself slide around his erect cock. Together with Jean Luc, we presented her to our members to be sucked in once more. Michel did not remain inactive, sometimes taking her by the waist to accompany her ups and downs, sometimes titillating her clitoris, but most of the time he grabbed her breasts, which he seemed to particularly appreciate and to which he gave a treatment that seemed to me rather manly but that his partner appreciated since she did not complain about it, sometimes his hand disappeared behind her back and seeing how Gisèle squirmed during these moments, it was obvious that he introduced one or more fingers into her anus.

Gisèle during this time offered us the sweetness of her mouth, while she masturbated us or caressed our balls, alternately she pumped us with enthusiasm, kissing, sucking, licking our tense cocks putting them end to end to lick the whole, and also on Jean Luc's injunctions she brought them closer, putting them well parallel and she stretched her lips and kissed both our penises. I could read in her eyes all the pleasure she was feeling and follow the progression of her pleasure that made her suddenly arch her back and throw herself backwards claiming her pleasure accompanied by Michel who intensified his penetration until the end of her ejaculation. The vision of this torrid pleasure triggered my own pleasure and I spread my cum half in my wife's mouth and half on her face.

Jean Luc, whose strength was still intact, made Gisèle stand up and then asked her to kneel, one knee on each arm of the chair and lean against it. He made her arch her back, asked her to raise her buttocks high and in this obscene position in which she shamelessly exposed her rump, he began to massage her separation and the eye of the scalpel that had begun to be dilated by his accomplice when he had announced his intention to fuck her. Without asking her opinion or mine, he began to soften the area. Once the orifice was enlarged, she presented the glans and began a slow but inexorable invasion.

Unaccustomed to the diameter, Gisèle winced in brief pain, but once the glans was past her features relaxed and Jean Luc completed his full length thrust. After a brief pause, he began a long back and forth motion into his partner's loins.

I found it deliciously degrading to see my wife lying in the chair in a particularly obscene position that only allowed her to open her thighs as wide as possible and endure the assaults of her partner drilling into her rump and swaying her breasts to the rhythm of penetration. With her mouth open she was now emitting little moans, clear signs of her pleasure that she finally took as well as Jean Luc who flooded her bowels.

Michel and Jean Luc who were still lusting after Gisèle were not anxious to see us leave, so we allowed ourselves a period of rest in which we quenched our thirst while kissing and caressing our partner who asked for just that and returned kisses and caresses. The caresses became much more intense and penetrating and we began to feel a slight erection again. After exchanging a wink with Jean Luc, Michel declared without worrying too much about me:

Now we are going to make you a sandwich.

Gisele gave me a shocked look - obviously we had seen this situation in R-rated movies and for her it represented one of the heights of perversion, and that she absolutely wanted, even if she was afraid of it, to try the experience. But now her back was against the wall and she was screaming:

It's not possible, I've never done it and you're too big, you'll tear me apart.

But no, you'll see, we do it to everyone we do each other, they liked it, and besides, your little hole was a little bigger, right?

Yes, it was, in fact, I felt it go through when you sodomized me, listen, I want to try, but you promise to stop if it hurts too much, right Philippe, you'll tell him to stop'.

I nodded and Michel continued

'Ok, whatever, I'm sure with a fucker like you there will be no problem, you will cum like you have never cum before' and added to my intention 'they are all the same, you will see, your wife as well as the others, real vicious girls'.

Jean Luc lay down on his back and asked Gisele to come on top of him. She straddled him and let herself slide on his sex, while Michel positioned himself at her side and gave her his to suck 'so that it was stiff'. Michel had her bend forward until her breasts pressed against Jean Luc's chest, who arched her back and grasping the fleshy globes of her buttocks in each hand, spread it wide to free her already dirty anus, which was still a little glowing. Michel took position and guided his cock to the edge of her rectum and began to introduce himself. Apparently it was not easy because Gisèle asked them:

Slowly, slowly, it's burning, stop me while I blow, yes like this, go ahead and start again slowly, you're so big.

Which they did, commenting

You can see they're in there, you're up to your balls, can you feel them?

Oh yes I can feel them, they are huge'.

'Now we're going to move, you're going to like it'.

They asked her to lean on her hands and they began to move, alternately, tuning their rhythms, as one went deep inside her, the other came out to the glans and the movement resumed. I felt like watching a pornographic movie or a daydream: before my eyes I could see my wife, who was wearing a garter belt, offering herself to a double penetration even in front of the cocks that were tugging at her. Very excited, I approached her and pushed my penis into her mouth. Under the blows of the cocks she often released my sex, understanding, I did not insist too much letting her breathe contenting myself for the moment to present her a few moments then caressing her face.

The pleasure that had long since given way to the slight pain of the intrusion was progressively intensifying, her two partners were taking advantage of it to accelerate their rhythm, their hands were going on her, their mouths were resting on her body, Jean Luc had taken possession of her breasts and was licking them or making them protrude, biting her erect nipples. Gisèle, sweating, was panting with pleasure, sighing and moaning:

Look what they are doing to me, it's terrible, oh yes, they are filling me completely, aaah, I feel them sliding against each other, oh it's so good, look they are fucking me and fucking me at the same time, it's so good, yes, will I leave soon?, yes?, more?, harder, aaaah yes fuck me?

Of course they didn't hesitate to respond favorably to the request and in a long complaint Gisèle came noisily, offering her orifices to the cocks that were filing her. The two lovers let her recover for a few moments and then resumed their penetrations. Quickly Michel, well sheathed, announced his pleasure and ejaculated in the annular duct he was occupying. As he pulled out, he said:

'Your turn, go ahead, the place is hot'.

Trembling with excitement, I positioned myself and inserted my penis into her open anus. Penetration was incredibly easy, facilitated by the previous intrusion and the emission of Michel's semen that served as a lubricant. What a sensation! Through the thin wall I could feel Jean Luc's sex sliding against mine and unleashing waves of pleasure in Gisele. I warned that I couldn't last long and Jean Luc responded:

I couldn't last very long and Jean Luc replied, "Anyway, neither could I, it's going to go away."

He pulled out of Gisele's soaked vagina, knelt in front of her and pushed his glistening cock into her mouth. She didn't have time to suck him as long as he announced:

So, so, open your mouth and stick out your tongue.

And he ejaculated long on her outstretched tongue and face. In turn, with my hands clasped on his hips, I let my pleasure flow into the loins of my offered wife.

As we toasted one last time Michel and Jean Luc complimented Gisèle on her 'cock talent', and after lavishing her with a few caresses and kisses, we took our leave exchanging our phone numbers, Gisèle still dressed only in her shirt but this time with her face stained and her groin sticky with cum.

After our second adventure, Gisèle's evolution continued. She told me that she had experienced incredible pleasure and that she wanted to do it again if I still agreed, maybe even with whoever had made her want it. I confirmed my agreement by telling her how exciting I found it. Since then, always carefully combed and made up, now habitually wearing high heels, deep cleavages that offered a view of her breasts, decidedly shorter skirts that made men turn as she passed, she was beginning to discover how much she enjoyed this disturbed pleasure caused by the more or less lecherous looks placed on her. Sometimes she neglected to wear her underwear when she went out, which of course I encouraged her to do. A third adventure contributed a little more to Gisèle's perversion. I was at work when the phone rang around 9 o'clock.

It was Gisèle, panicking:

Philippe, I just got off the phone with Michel, they want to come here with Jean Luc.

What, when?

Now they said they're going to be here in half an hour and that I have to get dressed, I mean naked, and that we can do without you, and that they'll let me pass until you come back, what am I supposed to do?

I don't know, do what you want."

'Yes, but you're not here, it scares me, and then this way I'll feel like I'm cheating on you?

'Listen, after the other day, there's no point, I know you want it and then you'll tell me.'

'Without you I would never dare'

That's completely absurd, I'm sure you're dying for it, if it's my permission you want, well go ahead, there it is. In a way, I want to find out if it is exciting to know that your wife is being jumped by two men? In the absence of her husband.

Are you sure, if that is what you really want, you will be a cuckold my dear, I will let them do what they want'.

What a vicious woman you are. All that's left for me to do is to wish you a good day my dear, see you tonight at 6 o'clock."

She rushed to the bathroom to put on her makeup and only had time to put on a pair of thigh-high stockings when a car pulled up in front of the house. With her heart pounding and stomach clenching as she slipped on her stilettos, she heard footsteps crunching on the gravel of the driveway. The expected and dreaded ringing sounded. A split second of hesitation and Gisele opened the door, Michel and Jean Luc were there. Contrary to what she had thought, they did not throw themselves on her, they kissed her neck, simply touching her breasts, pubic area and buttocks. Then they asked her for coffee. As she did so, a little surprised at the turn of events, they undressed. He found them naked, sitting side by side on a couch. When he served them, they asked her to get on all fours on the living room table, with her buttocks facing them and her thighs spread as wide as possible. What were they going to do? Jean Luc stood up, spread the lips of Gisèle's sex to open it, then seeing a candlestick on the fireplace, he grabbed the candle, smeared it with saliva and without further ado pushed it into her anus.

The two men, drinking their coffee, commented in grave terms on the spectacle offered: open thighs, open pussy, candle inserted between the buttocks? and began a curious interrogation.

Are you happy to cheat on your husband?

I don't know

How can you not know, what about us, what's the problem here? Come on, do you like it or not?

I think so, yes

"Do you think or are you sure?

'I am sure'

"I am sure of what

"I'm sure I'm happy cheating on my husband,' she repeated.

"Does it excite you'

"'Yes'

"What turns you on?

"What you're going to do to me

'And what we're going to do to you'

'Whatever you want.

Do you want to be fucked?" asked Jean Luc

'Yes' she answered

'You're not going to answer yes or no every time, just say it' scoffed Michel

So?

Realizing that in reality these questions were only intended to make her say crude words and cause her humiliating excitement, she answered

Yes, I want to be fucked.

Well, there you go, you've succeeded. In what position?

Doggy style, that's my favorite position'.

'You know what doggy style is.'

'Erm! Yes, it's the female greyhound'.

'So?'

I want to be fucked doggy style. Like a bitch in heat' she continued obediently

'Is that all? And after I fuck you?

I'll suck your cock.

"How?

'Good and hard, I swallow it all.'

"And then

I'll masturbate you between my tits.

'That's a good idea, but you don't say breasts, you say tits, tits, tits?

'I'll masturbate you between my tits'

'Cool and then what?'

'And then you will fuck me'

You like to be fucked

'Yes, I like to be fucked by a big cock'.

'And in a sandwich you like it?'

'Oh yeah, I like it, you know I like it, come on, I can't take it anymore'.

'Don't worry, you'll get some cock, but you'll have to be very slutty.

I promise I'll be a great whore, I'll do anything you want...' she capitulated after hesitating for a moment

Michel said to Jean Luc

'Well, since he's in a good mood, our little slut, let's do it.

They stood up, Michel took the candle from its sheath, not without going back and forth, saying:

It's only a postponement, we'll put you bigger later."

They made him put one foot on the ground to spread his legs, then Michel caressed for a moment the offered slit of the glans and asked:

Do you want it?

Oh yes, put me there, put your big cock inside me, I'm waiting for this," she replied.

Jean Luc, not wanting to be outdone, walked around the couple and presented his penis to Gisele's lips, which were rounded around the gag. The fact that Gisele was once again being taken by two partners, moreover in her own living room and without her husband, gave her a very strong feeling of arousal that resulted in the ardor of her fellatio and the unrestrained offering of her pussy that Michel filled at length while stroking her groin. The two men noticed her total availability and began to comment on her impertinently:

Can you see how she likes it without her husband?

See how she likes it, see how she sucks me?

She's soaking wet, the slut! My cock is soaking wet, she's squeezing, oh boy, she's going to cum, the slut."

Indeed, Michel's long mental preparation and thrusts triggered a brief but violent orgasm in Gisèle. Then Michel gave way to Jean Luc who in turn penetrated her soaked sex and grabbed his partner by the breasts. Michel too, hooking his fingers in her hair, ordered him to suck her, depositing his own secretions on her tongue. Several times, men changed places just when their partner was about to reach pleasure, thus making him decrease to start again. Jean Luc, who at that moment was getting sucked, grabbed her by the hair and said:

Come on, suck, I'm going to throw the mash."

And he burst into whitish jets that crashed onto Gisèle's face and lips, and she was finally allowed to reach pleasure.

Aaaah, yes, Michel, Aaaah this is good, put it inside me, yes, again, your cock aaaah further fuck me, fuck me again, is it strong aaaah? and she came with a scream as Michel in turn poured into her silky sex. He came out of her and asked Gisele to do a 'little job' for him, which she obediently did, tasting the mixture of juices. He sat down on a couch and asked her to continue the oral exercise so he could get off again.

'Wait, I'm going to the bathroom and I'm yours,' she said.

Why are you taking a bath?

I need to clean my groin a little bit" he replied

Absolutely not, today we want you dripping, dripping all over, Philippe can see that you have been given the job, that when you walk, you stain the tiles with what comes out of your mold and your ass, come on, you wanted to give me a Spanish hand job, come on.

Gisèle blushed, understanding that her lovers were not willing to play games and that they took a mischievous pleasure in 'forcing the dose' to make her feel that she was at their mercy and that they intended to take full advantage of her. She obediently knelt down and took her breasts in her hands and squeezed the half-stretched member between her fleshy globes. The gentle treatment she was giving him resulted in a full erection and she alternated between massaging her breasts, vicious licks on his turgid glans and newly swollen balls, and kissing her lover. Jean Luc, during this time had not been idle, positioned behind Gisèle, caressing her shoulders, her back, her waist when her mouth was free, turning her head to kiss her at length pushing his tongue into her mouth as far as the position allowed. Gisèle responded passionately to his kisses, offering him her mouth, her lips, her tongue, knowing full well that he would not be satisfied. In fact, his hands were caressing Gisèle's loins, then her buttocks, and she thought 'here, I'm going to do it' when she felt a finger pressing on the still closed corolla. Quickly Jean Luc, digging into the previously tested sex, retrieved the moisture and cum flowing out, and busied himself lubricating the opening of her loins.

'Do you still want to be fucked?" he asked, inserting two fingers into the narrow shaft.

'Huummmm' she nodded, with Michel's penis in her mouth.

'Stop it Michael, let him express himself, so you still want to be fucked?

'Yes, fuck me, put me in, squeeze me with your big cock, my little ass is waiting'.

Well, you're making progress. You'll see, you're going to have a great time, you vicious slut, I'm going to fuck your ass, and we're not going to do it just once, you have a strong ass, can we do it several times?

'I told you I'd do anything you wanted like a real whore'.

Okay tomorrow, I doubt you'll be able to sit down."

Gisele shuddered, this was promising, the muscle was now dormant under the efficient work of the twin fingers. When she felt sex against her anus, she arched her back as if to better offer herself for penetration. This was not enough for Jean Luc who asked her:

I can't see your hole very well, spread your buttocks with both hands.

Submissive, Gisèle took her buttocks with both hands and spread them as wide as possible in this obscene attitude and simply said:

Come."

The intrusion was not long in coming and Jean Luc slowly penetrated her dilated rectum until Gisèle felt his testicles against her vulva.

'There, you're good, you know what you are?

A whore' she ventured

'Yes, but then again

A vicious girl taking it in the ass.

'That's almost right, you're a slut'.

'Yes, I'm a slut, proud and happy to be one' she replied getting into the game.

'Come on, use your mouth for something else than talking bullshit, pump my knot' Michel asked Gisèle who obediently obeyed realizing with pleasure that, once again, the two exits of her digestive system were receiving the homage of two virilities intensely hindering them.

Then Michel manifested a desire for change. Jean Luc came out of the shaft he was working on, sat down on the couch and enticed Gisele to come and impale herself on his erect manhood. Turning her back to him and spreading her buttocks she made contact with his lap and then slowly slid down his member.

Oh, this is good, this makes it even better," she moaned.

'You haven't seen it all,' replied Jean Luc who suddenly spread his thighs, which had the effect of spreading Gisele's thighs even wider and knocking her off balance backwards, stabbing her deep inside and making her lose her breath under the effect of surprise and invasion. The rest happened quickly, Michel, knelt down, spread the lips of her vulva and then began the introduction of his cock into the dripping cone. Given the importance of Jean Luc's presence, penetration was not easy. Gisele tried to make it as easy as possible for them, tipped backwards and firmly locked on the chuck, she gave herself as much as she could, opening herself as wide as she could.

'You're really tight today,' Michel told her.

It's Jean Luc's fault, he's too fat.

But no, you'll see, anyway he has to adapt", he continued.

You're right, go ahead and push it in, oh it's huge, it's going in, put it all in' she said feeling her orifices expanding up to the diameter of the two machines.

Well that's it, that's it, that's what you wanted, right! Both of them at the same time?

'Yes, Yesi, now take me hard'.

Responding to the injunction the two men tuned their pace, then began to rake hard. One hand on Jean Luc's hip and the other on Michel's shoulder, offered to the sexes that hammered her, to the hands that caressed her, to the mouths that took hold of hers, she abandoned herself completely, following carefully the slow increase of pleasure that her two lovers offered her without any concern. The ardor that the two men put into her soon bore fruit and from that moment on it was nothing but moans and groans, as their members alternately entered and left the twin sheaths of Gisèle who had a first noisy orgasm, then almost immediately after a second that led to the release of the pleasure of the two companions who remained inside her, breathless, until their penises had lost their strength.

Did you enjoy it more?" asked Michel.

Oh yes, it was terrible, you make me reach a crazy pleasure' she answered.

You'll want to do it again with the roles reversed.

'If you like it'.

'Of course we do, but do you want to?

Yes I want, I told you, of course I want, you are making me cum like it's not possible, and besides, I already told you I will do anything you want".

'Well, okay, in the meantime make us something to eat so we can regain our strength'.

She complied under their lustful gazes and still naked except for her stockings prepared a quick snack, with a strange feeling of both emptiness and spread of her vagina and rectum that were gradually returning the juices they were full of and slowly beginning to flow to her thighs.

Sitting between the two men, the quick meal was the pretext for hand kisses and many caresses on and in Gisèle's body, who responded by manipulating their purse and masturbating the two penises that were regaining a fear of stiffness. Towards the end of lunch, after rummaging through the refrigerator, they had her get up and lean against the table, inserted the end of a cucumber into her pussy and masturbated her anus with a carrot, saying:

Next time buy two cucumbers, we'll put both in you.

This manipulation of the vegetables began to heat up all three of them, Gisele squirmed to facilitate the coming and going of the vegetables and the two men began to get hard again.

'While we drink our coffee, go make yourself a little more presentable,' Jean Luc ordered,

When she came back with her hair done and made up, they said.

When she came back with her hair done and makeup, they said, 'Well, you could have used more makeup, you're a little bland, make an effort, we want you to look like a whore, go fix it,' Michel continued

Gisèle turned back a bit, finding this request a bit abusive, but, tamed, she obeyed and it was with a lot of makeup that she returned, a bit embarrassed, but terribly excited. Finally she thought that if she had to act like a girl of few virtues, why not look like one too. This thought made her even more excited.

Ah! That's more like it. Come on, that's not all, or she's in your room so we can take a nap' said Michele.

Gisele looked at them, puzzled and questioning.

'Don't worry, your nap will be restless' Michel reassured her.

They carried her towards our room, made her lie down between them and then started petting her again. Placing them on either side of Gisèle, they began licking her breasts, then sucking her nipples, which had become stiff from the effect of the licking. Her breasts being a very sensitive erogenous zone for Gisele, this practice quickly heated her up and manifested itself in a ripple in her hips that both men noticed immediately.

You're getting wet, aren't you slut?" said Jean Luc.

Yes, I like what you do to me

And you like it' they asked again as they began to nibble on her nipples.

Oh yes' she replied as she arched her back.

Then they began to masturbate her, Michel inserting without difficulty two fingers in her anus and Jean Luc two other fingers in her slit that remained open, while he solicited with his thumb the stinging clitoris. Under these various expert actions Gisele once again quickly reached pleasure. Her two lovers positioned themselves on their knees over her face and held their spines out to her, asking her to lick them, which she did with all the voluptuousness of which she was capable. Satisfied with their erections they said to her.

'Come on, what is promised, what is due, get into position, get on Jean Luc'.

She straddled him, crouched over the member with an eager gaze, then grabbing it at the base, she let herself slowly slide around it, making Jean Luc sigh with ease. Then knowing very well the next step in the program they intended to reserve for him, he knelt down and then leaned on his hands, raising and lowering his pelvis so that his penis occupied well into the depths of all the space offered. Jean Luc took each of her buttocks in his hand and spread them as wide as he could, exposing the entrance to her loins, still flushed and a little open from the previous strains. Holding her breath, Gisèle arched her back, waiting for the next step.

She understands quickly, now, no need to draw her a picture.

Go fast, don't make her wait, put her asshole in.

She felt Michel place his glans against the open corolla, then he introduced himself, this time without difficulty into the distended mucous membranes. Without giving her a break, they began to give her a big thrust, encouraging her:

Go ahead and do your best, here we go, get your ass in there.

'Yes, move, we will fuck you, we will make you scream, you can feel our big cocks'.

'Yes I can feel them, they are huge, you are filling me with your big cocks, it feels good'.

'You love it, don't you bitch'.

'Yes, I love it.'

And they resumed their assaults, which became more and more violent as they noticed the evolution of their partner's arousal. Gisèle did her best to offer herself, feeling their sexes slide freely through her. Faced with Gisele's reactions, they became more brutal, Michel clasping his hands in the flesh of her hips and weighing heavily on her loins to make her arch as much as possible. As for Jean Luc, he had grabbed Gisèle's breasts and was kneading them without delicacy, not forgetting to chew on her nipples on which he was pulling, pinching and twisting to the limit of pain.

Gisèle, drenched in sweat, her orifices ravaged, groaned and gasped as she felt a brutal pleasure coming.

Then she sank, much to the delight of her lovers, into a kind of verbal delirium interspersed with onomatopoeia:

Aaaah, yes, more, more, aaaah my breasts. you're hurting me! continue yes, grope them again, I'm so horny aaaah bastard, what are you putting on me, still give me your cocks aaah hard, yes fuck me with your big cocks, yes fuck my pussy, Michel burst my ass, aaaah I'm about to cum, it's hard again, ah bastard, fuck me and fuck me, or fuck me and fuck me like a whore, yes I'll be your whore, give me your juice, I'll do you all, I'll suck you, yes even what is my ass, again, harder, fuck me hard! aaaaaaah' and with a quivering of her whole body she started a long orgasm with a scream and then collapsed on Jean Luc's chest. When the spasms of pleasure subsided and she resumed breathing Michel and Jean Luc got her up and expressed their desire to be able to cum in their turn. She asked them:

Yes, but go slow at first, everything is sensitive everywhere, if you go gradually I think I might cum again.

We'll do what we can," Jean Luc retorted, then with some consideration, they began to file her in rhythm, first slowly so that she could fully enjoy the goads that penetrated her in turn up to the guard, then progressively going in a crescendo, so that once again she was on the launching pad of a new orgasm that her partners controlled so that she could fully participate. When the three were at the end of their endurance, they broke out into a concert of sighs and moans, interspersed with crude and even vulgar language. Gisèle once again, under the effect of pleasure, flooded the member that was smashing into her pussy with its streams, felt the rods swell inside her and then flood her mussel and her bowels almost at the same time. The two men, also sweaty, withdrew from the burning sheaths with a curious wet hiss, sat her down on the edge of the bed and presented her with their still stiff and slimy members.

Did you want to suck? Well, go ahead and suck, your whore's tongue will be perfect for nickeling us," said Michel, whose penis was protruding from Gisele's butt.

He hesitated for a fraction of a second, then closing his eyes he embraced the first sex, then the second, taking turns on his tongue to collect the curious mixture of his own emissions, their covered tassels, and the last drops of semen dripping from their flesh. They surrounded Gisèle more tenderly to cuddle her gently, telling her:

It was great, you were really great, did you enjoy it? With a sigh she answered

Oh yes, I've never had so much fun, but I'm ashamed, I feel like I acted like a pig.

Of course you acted like a pig, and a real one? We loved it, to see you, we wouldn't have believed it, underneath your preppy or almost preppy look is a fun slut' replied Jean Luc.

I don't have to be the first one' he replied

'It's true you're not the first, but we have a lot of fun with you, there aren't many who like it as much as you do, you're made for it' he replied.

Besides, if you agree with you, we will satisfy all our desires, Jean Luc is right, you are made for this, we don't know many who get turned on like this, you will see, we will introduce you to friends so that they can make you do even dirtier and vicious things.

If you want, I can't resist, you turn me on too much," he admitted.

As if to seal the pact, they kissed her for a long time, one after the other, and proposed to run her over at the same time once again.

No, that would be too much and my anus is a little sore.

You're right, you shouldn't overdo the good stuff, especially since you have to save it for Philip.

After freshening up, they went back to lying down and the two men decided to take care of Gisèle. With sweetness and skill, they caressed her, kissed her all over her body and then made her legs spread, took care of her groin with their mouths. Michel took care of her clitoris, which he sucked and then titillated with his tongue, while Michel used hers as a little sex making it go back and forth in her vagina and sometimes even in her butt. Obviously under this gentle treatment she allowed herself to float to a new orgasm.

Then Michel asked her what time it was:

What time does Philippe get home?

He told me around 6pm.

Oh, then we have to organize, he has to have a good picture of his wife when he arrives, go put on lipstick and come to the dining room.

She obeyed, then joined them. Jean Luc sat her on the dining room table, slightly tilted, with her breasts hanging down so they could swing freely, he made her arch her back, spread her legs and stood behind her saying:

As soon as we hear the machine, you stand like this, I will fuck you and Michel will put his cock in your mouth so Philippe can see you in action.

Again, without knowing why, she obeyed again and when I entered it was the vision of my wife, her body marked with red marks, witnesses to the hard caresses that had been lavished on her, sucking one while the other sodomized her, that struck me with full force. I approached and Michel said to me as he withdrew from Gisèle's mouth:

'Hi, come say hello if you want'.

I leaned in and kissed her. I then noticed that the underside of her face was stained with slimy spots and streaks and her mouth gave off a strong smell of semen, evidence of some of her activities during the day.

Somewhat mockingly Jean Luc said, 'We've prepared her a bit, come and take her ass.'

A little prepared he said, her whole groin and the inside of her buttocks was as if covered with a shiny film, her sex from which a mixture of chypre and cum was flowing was scarlet and still gaping but it was especially the sight of her crimson anus, wide open and swollen, which was also returning in whitish rivulets the evidence of the pleasure experienced by her lovers that was impressive; she had not spared herself and had not really been bored. Quickly I let go of my pants and slipped it through this enlarged orifice without difficulty. During this time, Jean Luc and Michel presented her with their lives which she used to alternately masturbate and suck. I noticed that she hadn't thought for a moment about pulling away from the one who had been sucking her guts earlier, and Michel replied with surprise;

Just now he proposed it to us."

I was stunned, he must have enjoyed it? Too excited to contain myself I flooded my wife's loins. Jean Luc and Michel made her kneel on the floor and ordered her to 'give a good blow job' which she did conscientiously until she ejaculated on her tongue, face and even her breasts.

Afterwards they told me what a great day they had had and how Gisele had lived up to it:

She was perfect, in fact, if you'll allow us, we'd like to do it again from time to time, Gisèle is meant to be shared, we're thinking of doing and having her do many things, even lending her to friends or strangers.

I thought it was a bit too forceful with 'friends', but I replied, 'Gisèle already has my permission, if she doesn't agree, no problem'.

'Of course she agrees, she told us before,' said Jean Luc.

I looked at Gisele, amazed, she lowered her gaze and nodded her head, blushing.

Don't be so shy, you were less shy before, tell your husband you want to fuck again.

'Yes, that's right, I told them I agreed' she replied.

'The proof, here it is, a present for you,' said Michel, handing me a tape of a dictaphone they had hidden and turned on at the right moments, and added ironically, in front of a red-faced and ultra-impressed Gisèle, 'You'll hear what your little whore wife is capable of.' And this is another story?

At that moment, we were convinced that we were at the foot of a diabolical ladder, the passing of each rung of which would be synonymous with debauchery, as the rest would soon prove.

A SPECIAL COUPLE

My name is Didier, I am 40 years old, and I have been living happily with my wife Jeanne for almost 20 years. Jeanne is 46 years old. She is what you might call a beautiful woman, tall, well-fleshed out, with her curves in place. We form a modern couple where sexuality is very important, even if, as some will say, it's not like everyone else's. But before I tell you our story, let's take a step back about 30 years.

In puberty I had noticed that my sex was undergoing some metamorphosis, but I didn't know why, sometimes it grew and became rigid.

It took a summer camp to learn this by seeing some of my fellow campers who didn't hesitate to show off their attributes and fondle themselves in front of others. Seeing my ignorance, I was introduced to masturbation which, I must admit, I enjoyed immensely and at home I continued to practice it compulsively throughout my teenage years. Of course, I read a lot of dirty magazines and the sight of naked female bodies in obscene positions made me fantasize. Of course, I also fantasized about my high school friends, mentally undressing them and masturbating as I imagined them being subjected to my whims. But I was shy and my physique wasn't a stud, so I didn't dare get close to them. So I was a virgin, but it didn't matter, the masturbation was enough for me.

At home, my sister and my mother often went around with few clothes and even, when the weather permitted, did not hesitate to bask topless in the garden. From my room, discreetly, with the help of binoculars, I spied on them and the sight of their nipples and pubic hair, especially my mother's, poking out of their little bathing suits, gave me an erection.

I was a senior. That day, at that time, like every Friday, I was in study hall between French and math. This study hall was supervised by a young pioneer, Mademoiselle Rainier. I often passed her in the hallways of the school. She was small, slender, soberly dressed with a casual physique, she went unnoticed, she was transparent. When I say supervised, that's a big word because, at our age, we were no longer unruly children. As usual I sat in the back of the classroom with no side neighbors and, under the cover of a school notebook, I had hidden an erotic magazine. Of course I had an erection and my hand was tucked into the waistband of my pants. With my fingertips I was irritating the glans. This gesture lasted about ten minutes and then the desire to cum caused me to push my hand into my underpants and masturbate.

That day, feeling the pleasure coming, I looked at the stage where Miss Rainier was standing. Our eyes met. She was looking at me. For how long? I didn't know but, caught in the act, I decided to play the part of the one who, sure of himself, had nothing left to lose and so I continued my caresses. Then, I thought, she only sees my arm moving, she shouldn't know what my hand is doing in my pants.

So I continued to masturbate, looking at her with a slight smile. To my surprise she met my gaze and smiled as well. For the first time a woman was interested in me and moreover while I was in an unusual position. Mrs. Rainier's eyes seemed to invite me to continue. God, it felt good. The pleasure mounted inexorably and when I saw one of her hands disappear under the desk, I began to imagine her fingers digging into her soaked intimacy. At this point I was cumming and Miss Rainier must have realized it because she passed a greedy tongue over her lips but kept her hand under the desk for a while longer. The girl seemed to tremble, then her hand reappeared and, still staring at me, she licked her fingers.

What had just happened was beyond comprehension. As a result, the erotic magazine in front of my eyes looked very bland. The end of the study was coming. I didn't know what attitude to adopt. Should I approach her, I thought? But I was still too shy and left the room without saying or doing anything. God, what an idiot I am.

I was obsessed with what had happened. Several times I passed Mrs. Rainier and every time I tried to catch her eye, she lowered her gaze. Maybe she was as shy as I was. So I decided to write her a note and put it in her mailbox in the teacher's lounge.

When she discovered my message, this is what she read.

***

Dear Miss,

For the past week I have been thinking only of you. It seems to me that the show I unintentionally gave you wasn't too bad for you and I really liked yours. Since that day, your image has haunted all my nights and I can only fall asleep after remembering the memory of your hand slipping under the desk and, as you can imagine, after freeing myself from the tension that such memories can generate.

I don't know what attitude to adopt towards you and my shyness prevents me from approaching you, so I propose that we meet at the public library next Tuesday at 3:00 p.m., knowing that you are available that day. Please know that your absence at my meeting, which I would obviously regret, will let me know that you don't want to go beyond this wonderful time we have had.

Sincerely, Didier M. '

***

On Tuesday I waited for her in the library, until 4pm I was hoping but she did not come and the next day I found myself in the study room hoping she would be there. In her place was a token. Once again I was disappointed but I was about to go back to my old habits and rummaging through my bag to pull out an erotic magazine she entered the room, walked over to the pawn, talked to him for a few seconds, then walked over to me and without a word, put an envelope on my table and then left the room.

Dear Didier M,

I'm sorry I couldn't make it to your appointment, despite my desire to do so, but, as you rightly said, my shyness prevented me from doing so. Even writing, as I have just done, I have great difficulty in freeing myself and yet I am obliged to admit that I too enjoyed what happened that famous day and that since then my nights have certainly been as restless as yours.

If you still want to, we can meet tonight after school. I'll be waiting for you at the bar in front of the school.

Your obliging Jeanne R.

* * *

My heart started racing as I read this note. Of course I will go on this date. I have to admit that Jeanne, since that's her name, in the shy people competition, maneuvered finely. It's obvious that in a meeting, it's easier for the person waiting than the person arriving. No matter, let's be fair.

The two hours of class seemed endless. I couldn't tell you what topics were discussed. I left the school, crossed the street and entered the cafeteria. I was surprised that, despite her shyness, Anne had the audacity to greet me so that I could spot her among the many customers. She had chosen a discreet corner, a cubicle of sorts. She was sitting along the wall, on the skai bench, I took the chair across from her. To put on an act she called the waiter over and asked me what I wanted to drink.

- A mint diabolo, please, I'm very thirsty, I said.

- 'Two,' she told the waiter and then looked at me, 'I'm very thirsty too.'

We remained silent until our drinks were served and then we each took a sip. As we put our drinks back down each of us tried to talk at the same time. We burst out laughing. The atmosphere is relaxed.

- Go ahead," I said.

- No," she replied, "you go ahead.

- Well," I began, "it's really awkward to talk about it, but the reason we met was to discuss it, right?

- I can't wait to hear what you have to say.

- Well, there, I said it again, what you took the other day I do regularly. What you don't know is that during this study hour, instead of reviewing, I consult some pretty risque magazines and, you know how a man works, this kind of reading has certain effects on us that only certain gestures can soothe.

- Contrary to what you think, I don't know much about male mechanics and you, I suppose, don't know much about female mechanics, but I don't think the effects are very different and the method of relieving is little different.

- You are certainly right, also, at the same time, or at least assuming so, seeing you act in the same way seems to show that the female gender can have the same impulses. Unless you are the exception that proves the rule.

- Obviously, I can't answer for my sisters, but I don't think I'm unique.

Then, I started talking about me, my childhood, my adolescence and with more or less imaginary but never vulgar words or phrases, I made her understand that I was a virgin, that my sexuality was summed up in masturbation, that I liked it and that it was enough for me.

Jeanne had listened to me with great interest without interrupting me.

- So," she said finally, "if I understood correctly, you can do without women!

- No! I almost shouted, not at all, I like women, otherwise why would I read erotic magazines? Why would I ask you on a date? No! What I mean is that the pleasures I offer myself in solitude bring me a lot of physical satisfaction, but if the glossy photos that feed my fantasies could be replaced by warm, animated bodies, in a word, if women or simply a woman would agree to share the existence of a man who loves only masturbation, I would be the happiest of men.

- So, in summary, to be fully happy it would be enough for a woman to witness your masturbation. But what would she get in return?

- I don't know. There must be women like me who have a particular sexuality. Women who, like me, find true pleasure only in self-satisfaction and who feed their libido by watching men fondle each other.

- And do you think I can be that kind of woman?

- I don't. You tell me. All I know is that you took pleasure in seeing me take pleasure. I'm not wrong, am I? Did you have an orgasm?

- Yes, Didier, may I call you Didier? Call me Jeanne. Yes, I admit, I had an orgasm but so far nothing proves that masturbation can be the only way to get pleasure. But, why hide it anymore, you were right, I am one of those women for whom masturbation is an inexhaustible source of pleasure. I too, but only at home, unlike you, read racy magazines where men show off their manly attributes in good shape and not just show them off. In fact, I love gay magazines because men are generously spoiled by nature. Sometimes I like to see a woman stroking herself.

- Jeanne, you are wonderful.

- That's it! Your compliment goes straight to my heart, and to reward you, I allow you to come and finish your mint jelly, sitting next to me.

I jumped up, pushing the table in my haste, and went to sit next to Anne.

- Well, dear Didier, what a rush! Why do you think a simple change of seat can be a reward.

- I think you want to show, by this gesture, that you are no longer afraid of me, and also that, despite my confession, you have some semblance of affection.

- There is some of that, but it's mostly because of your confession. I'm glad to finally meet a man who isn't trying to jump on you. But I also wanted to know, and I had a little idea when I saw you standing there, if our conversation had any effect on you.

- What effect, I asked innocently?

- 'Well, my dear Didier,' added Anne, looking at my zipper, 'the appearance of a bulge in your crotch.

I really had an erection and stupidly, by an idiotic reflex, my hand came to hide this prominence.

- There," he said laughing, "I find you in the same position as the other day in class.

Again, I had a stupid reflex and removed my hand.

- No Didier, do me a favor and put your hand back. Don't you want to?

- What, you want me to... Here... In the cafeteria?

- Yes, but discreetly, behind the table, like the other day at school. You're dying for it, the proof is that your hump has grown again. Come on, then! I promise you another reward, in the meantime I'll tell you about myself.

I was trapped but Anne was right, I really wanted this. I looked in front of me, the small wall of the box was hiding me from the outside world. I put my hand on my flap and my fingers compressed my sex.

- Like you," she continued, "my childhood went smoothly, and when I started school in the sixth grade, I had to become a boarder. There were four of us in the dormitory, three girls in my class and a tall girl of 17 or 18 who was the supervisor. The latter was already very feminine and didn't take any precautions when undressing, so we got to admire her generous breasts and the fleece that covered her pubic area. One morning my bed partner came to see me.

-Anne," he said, "didn't you hear the big girl's moans last night?

- No," I replied, "do you think she was sick?

- But no, silly, not moans of pain, but moans of pleasure, well, you know what I mean?

-....

As I remained silent and stunned, my friend realized that I was not sexually liberated.

- What do you mean you've never given yourself pleasure?

I confessed my ignorance and she explained how, with certain gestures on a certain area of our body, we could achieve wonderful sensations. Although doubtful about these revelations, I promised myself to pay more attention to what might be happening in our room tonight.

That night I made an effort not to fall asleep right away, and since my friend was right, I heard faint moans from the big girl's side of the bed. The faint glow of the moonlight allowed me to make out the bed she was lying on. I could make out, rather than see, her body stripped of its sheet and blanket. Between her thighs one of her hands was flailing. I thought about what my partner had told me. So it was true, one could get pleasure by caressing one's own sex. After a relatively short time, I saw her body arch into a slightly louder moan, then fall back inert. At that moment I turned my head to my partner's bed and there, to my amazement, I saw her making the same gestures as our supervisor but I saw her much better, her knees raised, her thighs spread wide, her hand active between them. I also heard a splashing sound and, as our matron had done, her pelvis lifted off the bed as she let out a scream that she tried to stifle as much as possible but was loud enough that I was concerned that our matron hadn't heard it.

I turned back to her and then, to my surprise, I realized she was looking at my classmate and then looked at me. It seemed to me that she was smiling. Everything went back to calm. The pleasure they had just taken seemed to have knocked them out, but I, rather irritated, was having a hard time finding sleep when, again, I heard moans. They'll do it again, I thought, but no, it was the fourth roommate who was having sex. So, of the four of us, I was the only one who had never masturbated.

Jeanne paused in her narrative. My cock, which I was still clutching between my fingers, was hurting so much it was tense. Still on top of my pants, I began a slight jerking motion. Jeanne watched my hand move and smiled at me.

- I can see that my story has an effect on you," she said.

- 'I can't say otherwise,' I replied, 'but you, in all this?

- Can't you see that? Yes, I suppose I do, and yes, it was that night, when everyone was asleep, that I masturbated for the first time and, believe me, it didn't take me long to find the gestures and places necessary to reach orgasm and, given the pleasure I got from it, I knew, from that moment, that it wouldn't be the last time.

It was too much, too bad, at the risk of being discovered, I slid the zipper down and my hand grabbed my cock above my underwear.

- 'Didier,' Jeanne said as she saw me do it, 'you're going to masturbate right here in front of me and I'm going to love it.

Anne had said "yes" to me and more importantly she had used raw words. That turned me on even more. She continued:

- Your cock is big and hard, I would like to see it.

I agreed to her wish and pulled down the elastic of my underwear. My glistening glans appeared.

- Your cock is beautiful and I, Didier, you know I'm getting wet like crazy.

It was too much, a back and forth was enough to make me squirt. Anne went through her purse and handed me a Kleenex.

- You know you're the first man I've ever seen cum in real life? It's beautiful.

Watching me clean myself up, Anne removed two buttons from her skirt at the level of her pubes, which were buttoned up in front, and slid her hand inside.

- 'I know,' she said, 'that you'd like to see my pussy, but it's impossible here. Imagine it, open and wet, my clit swollen, my finger on it. Leave your cock out, I'll come, I'm coming.... Aaaah.

Anne pulled her hand out and showed me her glistening fingers. In my turn I handed her a Kleenex.

- Didier, my wanker Didier, how about I take you out to dinner tonight? I live within walking distance.

Of course I accepted the invitation. On the way to his house, he explained to me that throughout the school year, every night, the supervisor and his friend masturbated. At first more or less discreetly, then showing themselves clearly, and eventually they shared the same bed. They knew that the other girl and I knew, so they did nothing to hide and even seemed to enjoy our role as voyeurs, knowing that their performance would force us to masturbate, which we did, but with much more discretion. The strange thing was that it remained unspoken. No one talked about it. We acted by mutual agreement, each satisfied with the role he was playing. That's how the taste for so-called solitary pleasures came to me and never left me. The next year I no longer had the same friends and the new ones were wiser, although I knew they masturbated, they never made a show of it.

We arrived at Jeanne's house. Her studio looked like a cozy little nest, tastefully decorated.

- 'Sit down,' said Jeanne, 'I will prepare a tray for the meal.'

I sat on the couch while she went to the kitchenette, out of my sight. Her story came back to me and I smiled. I couldn't help but squeeze my cock through my pants. Jeanne's voice reached me.

- Didier, if you feel like it, you can take it easy, we're not in a public place anymore.

I was surprised by her injunction. She had the gift of double vision because this request seemed to be an invitation to resume my caresses but without constraints this time. Too bad, I said to myself, even if that's not the point of her request, I want it too much and then it will surprise her, pleasantly I hope. I unbuttoned my underpants, opened the fly and pulling down my underwear grabbed my cock. Jeanne returned to the living room with her tray, saw me and smiled.

- Well, my little Didier, I see we understand each other even if only half a word.

She put the tray on the coffee table and then knelt at my feet. She watched my hand move back and forth on my stem. She seemed fascinated.

- 'Talk to me,' she asked, 'explain your gestures, tell me what you feel.

- You see Jeanne, I release my glans as much as I can, with my finger I take the small drop that forms and spread it all over the surface.

Now that it's well lubricated, I run my finger along the base of the glans and then linger on the brake. Aaaah... It's divine. Now I grasp my cock, forefinger on the brake and thumb at the base and begin with small strokes back and forth. Aaaah... I'm not far from exploding.

Jeanne looked subdued. She went from kneeling to squatting and spreading her thighs, she showed me her crotch that didn't cover her panties. The little vixen had certainly taken it off while she was in the kitchen.

- 'Squirt,' Jeanne ordered me, 'come!'

My hand job sped up and her words and the sight of her pussy triggered my orgasm.

- Come Didier, yes, come well.

Once I regained my spirit, so shaken by this orgasm, I looked at Jeanne who was sitting on the stool not far from me.

- How did you know I wanted this?

- It must have been a woman's intuition and then maybe because I was aroused too. All these memories made my blood boil.

- Jet did you take off your panties while you were in the kitchen? You really wanted to break me down.

- Not only that. I can tell you right now that while I was out of your sight, I gave myself a little hand job. I was so turned on that I came in less than a minute.

- That's not fair, Jeanne, you deprived me of the show.

- But it was just to start over, my boy. You know, a woman's capacity for pleasure is far superior to a man's. Under my skirt, my little pussy is all wet, just waiting for my finger and your eyes to offer itself the pleasures it demands.

In my turn, I let myself fall at Jeanne's feet. Immediately her skirt went up and her thighs opened.

- Look Didier, look at my pussy. A real wanker's pussy. Look at how my labia are developed and full of blood, look at my slit that is yawning and full of moisture, admire my clit that is as hard as a small cock. If I wanted to, your gaze scrutinizing me would be enough to make me come, but since this is the first time for me that a man has witnessed my orgasm, I jerk off.

Jeanne's fingers went into action with a dexterity that suggests many years of practice. I didn't see much. Jeanne was too eager to have sex. All I know is that at the moment of the final explosion, she was squeezing her large clit between her thumb and forefinger. But what I couldn't see that time was amply exposed to me during the night that followed. Jeanne was right about women's orgasmic abilities, because she must have cum at least a dozen times.

The following days, weeks, and months Jeanne and I had many adventures because we realized that the pleasures we derived from masturbation were increased tenfold if we carried out our passion in unusual places and situations. So, in addition to the little jobs we gave each other in class, we got into the habit of going to public gardens. We would locate a man or a couple of lovers, sit on the bench in front and begin to mimic the movements of masturbation and, each time our interlocutor did the same thing, then we no longer mimed but made ourselves come for real. When it was a couple, while we made each other cum individually, they usually stroked each other. Generally, after taking our pleasure and theirs, we would leave exchanging a knowing smile, thus thanking each other for the pleasures we had taken. We also went to the movies. There, in the anonymity of the darkness, it was easier to indulge our passion.

I passed my baccalaureate and married Jeanne the following year. One evening, when we had just made each other cum, we were lying down, full, and Jeanne asked me questions about my adolescence because, curiously, our confidences had moved from childhood to adulthood, hiding this period.

- Did you ever," she asked, "have any attraction to people of the same sex as yourself?

- You mean did I have homosexual relations?

- Yes, I read that boys had all, more or less, played pee-pee with their classmates.

- As I told you, I discovered masturbation when I saw some of my friends doing it, but at that time, even though some of them fondled each other, I never felt the need.

- Too bad," exhaled Jeanne, "I wish you would have told me. You know, before I met you, I was a fan of gay magazines, and seeing these cute guys masturbating, or even sucking each other off, put me in a trance.

- I'm sorry to disappoint you, but maybe I suddenly remember an anecdote that might amuse you. For my studies I had rented a small apartment with a roommate. He was two years older than me and studying at the university. We didn't have much in common, so we didn't particularly like each other or share our private lives.

One warm evening I was having a hard time falling asleep and went to the kitchen to get a glass of water. My roommate was on the couch facing the TV, I could just see his head sticking out. On the TV were pictures of naked guys in the middle of an orgy, masturbating, sucking and fucking each other. I stood there for a few minutes looking at the screen and although I don't have homosexual tendencies, I found the show quite arousing and started to get an erection. Then I moved forward a bit and there I saw my roommate, completely naked, masturbating. His cock was huge, especially compared to his rather slender build. He hadn't heard me yet so I decided to let him finish and took my cock in my hand to stroke it. Suddenly he ejaculated. It was a real firework both in terms of quantity and force of ejection. I was about to quietly return to my room when, turning my head, he saw me.

Stop it, Jeanne! How do you want me to concentrate, for the last 5 minutes you have been exposing your pussy to me and stroking it.

- It's your fault Didier, your story excites me too much. But go on, he saw you and he knows you saw him, so what?

- Out of modesty he covered his lower body with the towel he had taken care to bring to dry his excess cum and began to stammer words that I didn't understand. I asked him to calm down and reassured him that everyone is free in their sexuality. He thanked me for my understanding and explained that he was certainly gay but had never acted on it and was content with movies and masturbation. As he spoke he kept his eyes on my lower abdomen. It is true that I had not gone wild.

- Didier," he said, "I see that the spectacle I have unwittingly offered you has not left you cold. I don't know where your tastes are, we talk so little, but I have never seen you with a girl, perhaps you too....

- No," I replied brutally, "I'm not gay.

I explained to him how I lived my sexuality.

- Yes, I understand", he said, "our interests are different, but we do the same thing to lighten up.

- It's true," I agreed, "but I'd like, if you don't mind, to see your sex again, I was quite impressed with its size.

My roommate removed the towel. His sex appeared, but even though he was at rest, it was already unusually large.

- Of course," he said, "it's not in the same position as before.

- I may have a solution," I said, "so that he can regain his pride.

I pulled down my shorts, my erect cock appeared, I grabbed it and began to masturbate. My roommate looked at me and put his hand out to grab my cock.

- 'No,' I said, 'don't touch it, just look at it and jerk off.'

My roommate looked disappointed but did as I said. I was the first to cum too, to reward him I put my hand on his cock, close to his, my fingers were struggling to get around it but his skin was warm and soft. Then he withdrew his hand and it was my strokes that made him cum.

He thanked me and before we parted I let him know that this would be the only time we would touch each other.

- Too bad," Jeanne commented, "I would have loved to meet him and be able to watch you, see your hands masturbating, your cocks touching, your... Aaaah... This is going to make me come... Pull out your cock... It's hard my bastard... Aaaaah... That's it, I'm coming.

- But you, I asked her after she had recovered, you let me know that you didn't hate seeing pictures of women fondling each other. Did you ever have relations with girlfriends?

- No, never with girlfriends! Maybe because I never dared. Shyness I think, but I still have a kind of special homosexual relationship, I don't know if I can?

- Now it's too late to back out, you made my mouth water, you have to go all the way.

- Well, this was two years ago. It was the middle of July, my father had just died. My mother and I were also in a lot of pain, so throughout the school vacation period I decided to stay with her. My mother seemed inconsolable. It is true that since they met, they had been living a real love story. There was a real physical communion between them that had never weakened even after so many years, and the noises that reached me regularly from their bedroom testified to their perfect carnal understanding. During the first month, my mother couldn't stand sleeping alone so she got into the habit of sleeping with me. The first few nights there were no problems but, by now you know me, going two nights without stroking myself was already a lot and from the third night on, as soon as I had made sure my mother was sleeping soundly, I made myself come. From day to day, or rather from night to night, I masturbated less and less discreetly and what had to happen, happened.

- Your mother woke up, I said.

- Not really, replied Jeanne, I was attending to my button and you know now how sensitive it is, that it was quite stiff and I felt the pleasure rise when, at my side, I heard moans. I stopped stroking myself and the moans continued. No doubt they were coming from my mother's mouth. I turned to her.

- Jeanne, my child, don't stop, continue your caresses, let's enjoy together.

- But mother," I replied, "what are you doing?

- Like you, my child, your father is no longer here and my body is thirsty for pleasure. For several nights I heard you masturbating, until now I resisted but today it was stronger than my will, my sex demands its share of pleasure. Jeanne, you want, don't you, to have some pleasure.

My mother, during her monologue, had not stopped caressing herself, and feeling that warm body so close to me, made me forget that she was my parent, she was becoming a woman, any woman, with her desires, her cravings and I resumed my masturbation.

- It's nice, isn't it, my dear girl. You like it too, don't you? Do you do it often?

- Every day my little mommy. Yes, I like it and you?

- I do it often too, even though your father gave me many orgasms, I liked to masturbate and I did it since I was a child.

- Oh mother, I am your daughter. How do you do it?

- First I think of dirty things, then when I feel my sex getting wet, I dip a finger or two into my slit and then.... Aaaaah and then I... How about I show you instead?

My mother threw back the sheets toward the foot of the bed and we found ourselves lying side by side, our lower bodies naked, our legs spread, our hands between our thighs.

- Look at me," my mother said, "and let me look at you.

To do this, she knelt in front of me, I had her very hairy pussy next to my head. I could smell her feminine scent in heat. For a moment she showed me her pussy, holding it open with her fingers. Her clit was pointed, long and stiff. Then my mother began to masturbate, uttering words without following them. Her body went into a trance, and then suddenly she stiffened, a stream of chypre flowing out of her pussy. Her orgasm was long and intense, I was stunned. I forgot to stroke myself and when I resumed my masturbation, my mother had just recovered enough to see me cum as well.

You seem to enjoy my story my beloved Didier, you are as hard as a bull.

- How can you resist that my dear Jeanne. I imagine you and your mother, dripping pussies, clitorises at attention. As I stroke myself, it continues.

- Almost every night after that we did it again, and the nights when nothing happened was because we had gotten carried away during the day. All it took was for one of us to show a little nudity or say a few words for us to feel the urge, and as soon as one of us talked about having some pleasure, the other would join in as well, and we would push our clothes over our bellies, which were no longer cluttered with underwear, so we could get to work faster. Generally the pleasure came quickly and this could be repeated 2 or 3 times during the day. You can see why, on those evenings, we were wise, although very early in the morning, well rested, we often let ourselves go to practice our passion.

These revelations finally got the better of my control and I let out several spurts of semen.

- You were really under a lot of pressure," Jeanne concluded. 'I've never seen so much cum.

- Does it still last with your mother?

- Yes and no. I went back to school in the fall and out of sight, out of mind, as they say. At first we called each other every day and often masturbated each other while we did it. Every month, when I got home, we would kiss and tell each other the pleasures we had taken while masturbating, and this would end in a tête-à-tête, or rather a frenzied pussy-on-pussy. Then we would each return to our usual lives, I would meet you, my mother would find, during my absences, other poles of interest, and our semi-incestuous relationships would subside.

Jeanne and I often talked about the relationship she'd had with her mother and each time it excited me terribly. The day she introduced her to me, I thought she was very beautiful and desirable and imagining her masturbating in front of her daughter, I had a spontaneous erection. That night we slept at her house and that same night, after relieving ourselves with a good masturbation during which we were not stingy with our moans of pleasure, we discreetly went to listen, through the door of her room, to the moans of her mother who had not been able to resist her desires. I tried to convince Jeanne to join her and accept me as a spectator but she wouldn't. But, just imagining it made us horny again and we had to do our business there in front of the bedroom door.

And that's how Jeanne and I are now together. Our love of masturbation has never wavered. After completing my studies in sexology, I opened a counseling center. I must admit that my patients keep Jeanne and I from falling into a rut. Very few of them, when I talk about masturbation, dare not talk about it frankly and their confidences, which I record, serve to feed our libido. Now, thanks to the miniaturization of cameras, I have been able to convince some patients to do practical exercises in my office. With image and sound, Jeanne and I have beautiful evenings of pleasure ahead of us.

Oh, I forgot to mention that next week we will be spending a few days with Jeanne's mother who just turned 68. Jeanne, who confided in me that her mother, despite her age, had not yet given up the practice of intensive masturbation, was planning, to cheer up her old age, to bring along the video and audio recordings we have. She then confessed to me that all these years she and her mother had continued to play their little games and that it was time to join in. I finally had to turn 40 to witness the scene I had imagined 20 years earlier.